Leviathan

MELANIE MCCURDIE

Copyright © 2017 Melanie McCurdie

All rights reserved.

ISBN-13: 978-1974266340
ISBN-10: 1974266346

This is a work of fiction. Names, characters, businesses, places, events and incidents are either the products of the author's imagination or used in a fictitious manner. Any resemblance to actual persons, living or dead, or actual events is purely coincidental.

No part of this book, be it digital or hardcopy, may be reproduced or transmitted in any form or by any means, electronic or mechanical, including photocopying, recording or by any information storage and retrieval system, without written permission from the author

DEDICATION

This is dedicated to all of those who have suffered, or are struggling with domestic abuse, and those left to fill the space left by a loved one taken by another.

ACKNOWLEDGMENTS

As always, for Muse

For My Love, Tom. Infinity and Beyond

To Foggy McCorrigan; my friend, thank you for always lending your support, encouragement, friendship and grammar skills. You are a treasure

My thanks and undying love and gratitude to my sisters by heart - Carolyn Graham, Patti Beeton, and Kelly Brandsness - for their proofreading and perusal skills. You make my job that much easier. Xo

Greetings adventurer!

Before you begin, a few discretionary words:

Keep out of reach of children

Everything written from this point forward is to be considered snippets from my own twisted imagination and/or my own opinion.

The words that follow are not an official representation of any human, animal (warm blooded or cold blooded), extradimensional beings and/or biologically challenged individuals.

Actual offences or nightmares may vary from individual to individual. If conditions persist, stop reading. Some reassembly may be required. Batteries and weapons not included. Objects in mirror *are* closer than they appear.

Gratitude does not include tax, title, license or freedom from further subjection to bloodsauce.

Enjoy your read.

Melanie

Ces belles paroles que vous prononcez me couper avec les vérités de poison.

Eveline Hood

*These beautiful words you speak
cut me with poison truths*

1

I suppose that I should introduce myself, since you are going be joining us shortly for a meal anyway.

My name is Calvin Moon. I am 30 years old, single, much to my mother's chagrin, and until about a month ago, I worked as a caregiver at the Silver Wing Retirement Home during the day and as a freelance programmer at night, when I could get the work.

I attended Cypress Summit College and received a psychology minor, but so does everyone else. Cutbacks and a rash of sudden deaths at the facility caused the government to step in and shut it down.

Everyone lost out there, but most of all the residents, who in some cases had to be hospitalised. All my former co-workers complained and the like but the more experienced ones found work right away. The rest of us are walking the streets looking for a full-time job and taking other odd jobs in the meantime.

[margin notes: incomplete thought. complained about what?]

I found Angel by accident one night, while trolling the net for something that might be better than the crap they have on TV. It had been a long day, and I knew I should have felt more blessed to have at least part time work through a temp agency but my feet hurt and I was in a rotten mood. Netflix had nothing that I hadn't seen and porn was a bore, so I just kept scrolling through when a pop up window caught my attention just as I had been on the verge of closing it down my browser.

There was a woman; She looked like an angel and she was shivering in the middle of a strange apartment with padded walls, waving what looked like a knife around at nothing. She seemed crazy at first, and admittedly, I watched in humour at first, even laughing out loud once or twice until I realised that she was truly afraid of whatever she perceived to be there.

She spoke aloud with an attractive husk, honey over whiskey, as though she were speaking to someone in another room in a perfectly modulated voice that clashed badly with how she lived.

Honestly, that's why I didn't just ~~close~~ shut down the ~~window~~ internet and go to bed, that, and the fact that she was ~~hardly hard~~ was easy on the eyes. In fact, she was beautiful, creased and repaired in places, and obviously gorilla glued back together in others, but those flaws, made her even more so, intreging.

Slim, but not boney, and full breasted, with a face that could be frighteningly lovely, if not for the fear that widened her eyes too much and rimpled the small lines around her lips.

I knew that I shouldn't be observing her misery like some sort of loser living in his parent's basement, but I was lonely and she seemed so afraid. No-one should ever have to fall asleep alone, feeling that way. No-one should ever feel that they are alone and unloved, and so, even though Angel didn't know then that I was, or that anyone for that matter, cared outside of her pathetic four walls.

I couldn't abandon her, so I called the police with the information I had. They ended up dragging me in and interrogating my exhausted ass for five hours before they released me, they then promptly hired me, as what they called an *independent consultant*.

What a joke! All it really meant was that I get to sit at home on my computer and watch Angel from sundown to sun-up and try to gage where she was, who she is and what has her so scared that her location was all but soundproof.

It's all a terrible shame, watching this sadly gorgeous creature struggle, but what's somehow worse for me is that no-one can find her, except through this feed from nowhere. It seems so unfair and so, I stay up watching with her at night while the police uselessly run the feed through all sorts of face-recognition programs and inundate news and online media platforms with articles and clips of the video in hopes that someone might recognise her and reach out. So far, no one has.

Observing Angel fall to pieces while she listens to her voice messages every time she walks through that door makes me ache, and I want nothing more than to catch her in my arms when she sinks to the floor as though the voices on that machine are stealing her will to live. I wonder if they are.

There is nothing I can do to stop her pain and I know it, but it doesn't change the fact that it hurts her.

Leviathan

I wish I could help because her suffering is becoming agony for me too. If only she would give us a direction, a name, satellite coordinate, hell a pizza order - just anything, but all we have is her first name.

Angel

2

She said her name that first night while laughing to herself about what a joke it was that her mother chose to call her Angel. She sobbed slightly, spewing curses with her tears, laughing forlornly whilst she described ~~they~~ the way her mother spat on her and called her a d~~ae~~mon the day she left.

Angel laughed and it sounded like bells, all the while insisting that she is nothing at all like those "feathery goody-two-shoe~~s~~d freaks," and grumbling nastily under her breath about having to pluck at the delicate bits of fluff that fly from the back of her sweater as she ruffles in anger.

She can't see herself, nor the glow that shines in her eyes when she denies her own being, admitting only to remaining less than fallen. I find myself weeping a little, too, at the despair in that small childlike voice she uses to argue with herself, then yelling at her to stop when she beats her head against the padded wall as punishment.

So tough in the daylight hours, Angel falls apart as soon as the door closes behind her and she can loosen the bolts and relinquish the hold the mask has on her soul. She is so strong and brave, but she thinks herself weak and it hurts to see that she truly believes it. This a Angel has never been a devil nor even a lesser demon, but rather, the people around her were and apparently are.

Angel's nights are long and mainly sleepless, full of some sort of nameless agony that she keeps in a silver heart locket around her neck like a talisman.

Her hand is always half clutching it with a feverish reassurance that is as bleak as it is concerning. It must be of some significance, some importance to her that evades the rest of us, but I think that maybe it's a small part of the agony that she enjoys. A reminder.

Watching her, night after night as she helplessly huddles under several heavy blankets, wearing that old green cardigan that's seen better days, laying there with chattery teeth and tear tracks on her cheeks depresses me more than I already am.

I know that it's my job to listen to her confused mumbled ramblings that are little more than a wall to bounce her terrified thoughts from. I wonder, sometimes though, if a mirror would be kinder.

Last night, after returning from wherever she goes in the daylight hours, Angel made herself a small meal and then sat at her small table to eat alone.

Between bites she spoke almost absently about the dream that she had woken from in the night screaming. The notes left by my counterpart the night before are vague at best and state only that she had been screaming in her sleep at 2:36 am.

That's what I get for taking a night off. Angel has never spoken of her life before now except for the few discernible words that she can give sound to in the few hours of rest she gets, and those are normally while she is staring trancelike at the door. Even though she is completely unaware that I am here, I think in some way that she does and I always happy enough to listen to her ramble as long as she was speaking.

Tonight, once again, Angel sits at her small table with her eyes fixed on her plate, pushing her food around for a long moment before she says some things that shock me tremendously.

I'd never heard such a dead and devastated tone come from a human being in my life. It was so unlike her that I put down the can of soda I'd been about to sip from and picked up a pen.

Her throaty voice is the stuff of wet dreams and had it not been so full of self-loathing, it would have been impossibly sexy. But it is and the pens moves almost of its own volition Angel quietly speaks -

"I hated that laundry room from the second I walked through the door of that horrible place. It was never home. The one thing that I never could understand was why he nailed the door shut. I guess he knew that I couldn't escape if I was cornered."

He? There had never been mention of a man before tonight, let alone enough of one to warrant a *he,* with such an implied hatred.

It makes me uneasy and my hand shakes while making detailed notes of whatever she chooses to say, just in case. Angel nibbles at her plate like a child that has been chastised and forced to sit at the family table instead of in front of the television.

"Everything was right. The roast that he liked to call a steak was blue rare and the vegetables he insisted be *crisp but soft too* were just so and smothered in enough butter to coat an urn. Even that God awful beer he liked was there; a six-pack instead of just the one that ended me in emergency last time. Even the house was spotless; in fact, it reeked of the bleach he demanded I use daily for any and all cleaning.

I'd done nothing wrong that time. I've tried and tried to figure out what exactly it was that offended him so deeply, but I keep coming up empty. I think that maybe it was just me. The fact that I existed at all."

Nothing wrong *that* time," I thought aloud, "I doubt whether you were ever at fault for whatever blame the bastard cooked up as an excuse to use his fists on you, Angel."

Surely there were family and friends? Did no one care enough to see that she wasn't being harmed? What about them? Having grown up in a loving home, it is really and truly beyond me how another human could stand by and let another be beaten like that, never mind let it continue once they were aware. Maybe this man kept her isolated from those that did care, and surrounded her with those of his ilk. There are certainly enough cases out there to support it as a theory.

Our telephones ring at the same time. Angel shudders, sighing deeply and I about jump out of my skin. The Bossman calls on my end, and I half listen to her conversation while giving my supervisor the lowdown.

She is arguing lightly with someone on her end, and this conversation is making her smile tentatively. She sure is pretty when she smiles. Angel laughs lightly and agrees to get in touch with the caller the following week, but this time the smile doesn't reach her eyes. She is lying. Whomever this is, Angel has no intentions of calling them back.

3

We wrap up our calls at the same time, and both of us sit, staring at the phones in our hands before setting them aside. I return to listening to her horrific memories and Angel returns to her lonely diner for one, thinking that she is invisible and that no one hears her.

"I hear you Angel. Every word." Maybe I should make my meals at the same time and then it won't seem so bad, for either of us. Eating alone isn't exactly an appetite making activity.

"He was exactly on time, as usual, punctual to a fault and nothing seemed amiss. I mean, I learned how to anticipate mood by the way the door closed and there was nothing that made my radar ping. I peeked out of the laundry room door to ask about his day and the like, you know, normal people stuff, before continuing my task.

He answered too, after cracking the top on what promised to be a long night of wobbly pops. If he had been in a bad mood he wouldn't have answered at all and likely as not I would have received a sucker punch for my effort, just like every other time. It was my mistake, I guess, to assume that it was a sufficient greeting, just enough conversation to give me a moment to start the laundry machine and then join him at the table. I closed the lid and turned to see his angry glare barely an inch from my face. He just smiled and then I had no air or strength left to stand. It wasn't his smile that made me weak in the knees though.

The steak knife I'd left beside his plate was deep in my stomach and I just couldn't stay on my feet.

He let go of it and watched me fall on the pile of his filthy work clothes that I had been trying to wash, then - Cal -"

I froze with my hand on my phone. She said my name? I rewound the tape and listened again; No, I misheard, she said hell or something similar. I was shaking badly with rage. He stabbed her. Someone dared to injure that precious creature with the intent to end her. There should be hospital reports and police reports, somewhere.

I hit fast-forward and was relieved to see that she had simply sat, ate, and said nothing more while I panicked like a fool. It had given me a hell of a jump and I felt immediately bad when I saw her wipe the tears away with a frustrated swipe. "Come on sweetie, keep eating but talk too, okay?" I mutter at the screen, absently wiping the dust away that had accumulated there.

As though on cue, Angel lifts a spoonful of what looks like rice to her lips and I nod to myself. Good. She swallows mightily and sighs, then starts again.

"I was bleeding on his dirty clothing and he was yelling at me for making a mess, calling me worthless and telling me how much I deserved what was coming because I never learned. But I didn't *do* anything, not that time, and I tried to say so, with my palm up to show him the blood there and what he'd done. It worked last time, but he just laughed meanly and shoved me onto my back. I knew I was in trouble but this was new. He'd hurt me before, in that room, but it was limited to the damage his drunken fists would do or at worst, an incident with a beer bottle that he thankfully abandoned before it went too far. He'd never done something like that before."

"Angel! Went too far?" I shout at the screen aghast at her blasé expression, "Just tell me who, Angel. Give me his name and we will make him go away. I promise, just say his name."

Snarling this at a mindless monitor does no good whatsoever but at that moment it was all I had to work with. I probably would have cheerfully torn the bastard to bits and at least saying it out loud made it unable to take back. The Universe had my intentions and I believed them to be pure.

Angel shakes her head and take another small bite from her barely touched plate, chewing delicately in silence and that's how it stayed for the next ten minutes. I watched her eat and she stared off into space while she finished her supper with a trembling hand.

Whatever she had escaped from was traumatic enough for her breath to come in short huffs with the remembered situation.

I went to the bathroom to relieve myself and to splash icy water on my face.

It stung some, but the surreal sense of reality was now firmly back in gear and ready for the next round. Angel had cleared the table and washed the few dishes that she'd used. Nothing was amiss, just quiet and tense.

She flicked her eyes up and stared directly at me through the camera she didn't know was there, her eyes searing holes into mine with a smirk, and the intensity made other muscles flicker in response. I wish she wouldn't do that

4

"I was having trouble breathing, really fighting like when I had pneumonia but I knew better than to scream or cry. Only no sound at all would save me more damage than giving voice to it. Tears get you hurt more often than silence," she tossed out nonchalantly, stunning me once again when she drops her eyes.

"I was sure he was going to stand over me to watch me die, with that fascinated not-there stare when he dropped to his knees and crawled atop me. He straddled my hips, and pulled the knife out my tummy so slowly I thought I was going to lose my mind with the pain.

The blade caught on something inside me, probably a rib, and I felt/heard it drag past six notches before he finally yanked it free.

There was blood on the tip and when the blade pulled free, it made an arc that painted a perfect line on the foam tile ceiling and it glimmered there like rubies.

He was still straddling me and this time I could feel that he was aroused, and was getting more so while I struggled under him. It was difficult not to though, because he was bigger than me; heavier and just bigger. There was no way to fight without being sure he would kill me for certain but I panicked when his thick finger poked through the hole in my shirt and into the wound, then started smearing the blood around. The wound ached when his finger brushed the outside edge but I could live with it easier than having him penetrate the puncture again.

I really thought I could live with it and then he shoved two fingers into the hole in my gut without more than a huff that sounded lustful and wriggled it around while I could do nothing more than punch at his face and scream.

I don't know how long it went on, just that it seemed like forever and when he got bored with that he beat me senseless for daring to pass out. That was a no no and I knew it,"

I had to vomit and I bent down between my knees to vomit into the small trash can I'd left between my feet. What kind of person does that to another human being? Only a monster and this man that she had wound up with was well and truly that.

Angel is still again, just sitting placidly while I reel inside, trying to wrap my brain around the things she is saying in such an unemotional way. Its as though she is describing someone else.

Maybe she is, or maybe, to speak this way is the only way she can live with trauma that this sick fuck visited on her fragile form.

I thought I was all right, but what Angel said next made me bow my head and vomit again.

"I came back to reality unable to breathe, and I was clawing at my neck before I was really conscious, I think. I know my nails caught my skin because I have scars where I scratched at the chain that had been wrapped twice around my throat. It was so heavy and cold against my injured skin. The chain was new.

He'd beat me hard enough this time that my eyes were almost too swollen to open. That was new, too; he rarely marked my face after the first time that it was noticed and a neighbour called the police. We moved away shortly afterwards.

My shirt was stiff with blood, I hoped it was blood, but the way it was stuck to the wound inside gave me surety. It made me so angry that I could imagine the idiot writhing on the floor with the same knife he stuck me with hanging out of his asshole and his appendage that he was so damned proud of whirling in the blender; and he, that sad excuse for humanity, I could see him bleeding out onto that stupid white carpet he had to have.

It seemed like imagining his suffering was to bring him clomping back to the doorway where I really was trapped this time. I could smell the beer on his breath when he stumbled over the threshold and it was gorge rising when he leaned close to my stinging cheek. The air around him was so rank and spoiled that it made me want to barf. He tried kiss me, yanking hard on the chain when I turned my face and tried to back away.

Kissing someone so roughly that their lips bled was the only way he knew how and when he'd been drinking, his kisses were vicious. He actually laughed when he pulled away and saw my lips had split."

5

Angel stiffens and covers her mouth with her left hand when a faint knock on the door startles us both, and I watch, helpless, as she wraps her delicate fist around the haft of the same knife I saw that first night. She keeps on the counter for instances like this, I suppose, and she creeps to the door and peers through the small hole into the hallway.

She hisses and her fist tightens on her weapon when the knocker pounds a little harder, making the door handle rattle with the force. She crouches like a wildcat about to pounce, and I can hear the low whine under her fear when the handle turns once or twice in small half-moon frustrated motions.

"Jesus, where are you Angel? I can't help you if you don't give us some idea! Give me a clue!" I'm as bad as my father when he yells at the football game on TV. Get it together Cal, and pay attention!"

I slap my face twice and lean in close to the monitor to try to glean any hint as to where she could possibly be. There is nothing at all to show her location. Just nothing! Even the windows are covered.

"I knew you'd find me one day," Angel mutters, recoiling when a man's angry voice blasts my ears. I can hear her clearly and can only assume that there is a mic very close to her. Who the hell did this to her place? He must really be bellowing for it to be that loud. She drops from her crouch to her knees and quivers with her hands clasped behind her back and her head lowered, and I find this both worrisome and arousing.

The man is still hollering, and the frame on the door seems to be dangerously close to letting go. All that I can do is sit here and watch her wait for the lunatic to break down her door and slaughter her.

"I knew that you'd never let me be, you sick son of a bitch. It was too good to be true, the small amount of peace I'd found here." Her shoulders heave and I can hear the terrified sobs she is holding back. I wish I could kill him and hold her until she feels safe enough to smile again.

Angel shudders then slowly rises and straightens from where she had dropped, adopting a momentarily predatory stance with a snarl at the door before placing her weapon on the counter again. The hammering on the door is suddenly gone, and Angel sits back at the table, this time cracking a fresh bottle of tequila and pours a shot into the glass that had been sitting on the table earlier.

"Stabbing me and fingering the hole like it was my pussy wasn't deviant enough for you, was it? Neither was beating me until I couldn't see, or chaining me to that damned wall. Even carving your initials into my gut wasn't even enough. What I did to deserve you, I wish I knew. I only hope that someone cares enough to check on me, and if they find me dead, I hope they know it was you."

Frustrated, I slam my fist on the desk and walk away wishing to hell I'd never found her. How the hell can anyone check on a woman that no one knows exists? I take it back; Obviously, someone does, because her apartment is wired like the FBI was monitoring her. I need a drink and maybe a joint.

I hadn't had either since graduating from College but now seemed like a perfect time to pick up the habits again, and I was beginning my search for liquid painkiller when I heard Angel clear her throat.

"Calvin Harper," Angel whispers and my spine feels like ice when she says my name, then turns into magma when she speaks it again. "His name is Calvin Harper and he is from South Zenia." Finally! Impulsively I kiss the screen on her face and quickly text the information to my supervisor while Angel keeps telling me her story, hoping that they can find something

"It wasn't enough for me to be wearing his punch stains under my clothing, or that I that I had to stitch myself up rather than risk going to get medical care. That was also against the rules. If I went to the hospital, then someone would know and that wouldn't do.

Cal loved the idea that I had had to walk around with welts from that big high school ring he insisted on wearing on my breasts and pubic area. I was bloody and I hurt from my soul out but that still didn't do it for him.

It wasn't until he took the same knife he stabbed me with, and dragged its serrated edge along my cheek that I truly began to fear for my life. He had begun to carve his initials under the puncture in my stomach, and that's when he finally committed the act that I had hoped he would pass out before I had to endure.

When I screamed at last, he groaned, came on my thigh, then stood up and kicked me in the ribs and left. I wanted him to die but I had more important things to deal with. My body was black and blue and I could barely see, let alone move very far with that damned chain I was wearing, but none of that mattered.

What did was that the fool dropped his keys when he stumbled out and I needed to get away or I would die by my own hand. I couldn't take it anymore. Somehow, with slippery fingers and no sight, I found them and fiddled anxiously with the key until the lock snapped.

I was finally able to get out of the heavy chain. Forcing my eyes open was agony. Gods, it hurt so badly that I couldn't even cry, so I just sobbed for a few moments like a damned baby, and then slipped into some fresh clothing and slunk towards the front door.

I could see him slumped in his favourite chair, snoring. Of course; he was; he had gotten his rocks off, had a satisfying meal and beer besides. What else would he do? I could see the knife I'd used to slice his steak on the counter, waiting for my hand.

I grabbed it and sprinted to his side. Every blade in this house was sharp enough to amputate fingers easily, and I knew that I could cut his throat with no struggle or issue. He was sleeping and would've bled out before fully waking.

I could've cut his throat, should've, but I slipped the knife into my purse instead and lurched out the door.

I stole his car and left it with no gas on the side of the road near the bus stop two towns over and to the south. A nice lady going west gave me a lift into the next state and I could rest some while she sang with her beautifully harmonies along with the radio. When I woke up, that sweet woman bought me breakfast and a ticket to wherever I wanted to go. I chose here.

And he's found me, again."

6

Angel sits at the table and says nothing more, only pours from the bottle until it is empty. Then she opens another. Occasionally she sighs and looks towards the blanket covered window with longing. I had hoped that maybe she would tear it off but she only continues to drink.

Around 4 am, Angel stumbles to her bed, and lays on her back with her belly exposed. In the dim light, I could see the choppy scars of what appeared to be letters underneath a deeply puckered mark. He really did carve is initial into her skin, and if that was true, then the rest was likely as well.

I rubbed my eyes and guzzled some coffee while I watched her writhe and toss in her sleep, calling out a name I had never heard before. Who or what is Leviathan?

My replacement, Detective Taylor, stomps in unceremoniously at 7 a.m. waking me from a dead sleep at the desk. He slams the box with hot coffee, a bag full of cream and sugar spilled out and fell to the floor. His wife, Joslyn had been cooking and he had brought enough food to feed an army.

Gratefully, I inhale half of it while filling him in and giving voice to my concerns regarding Angel and the events of the night before, expressly the story she told and the confirmation of such scars on her body.

Taylor just shook his head and wondered aloud if the man would have wanted his mother or sister to be treated that way. I suspect that they were; after all, children usually learn what they live.

I hand Taylor the file with my notes after extracting a promise that he would pass it on to our supervisor immediately, then head upstairs to the bedroom, exhausted. I need more sleep but I doubted that I would do much of it as I climb the stairs. How could I after a story like that?

Staring at the ceiling for what felt like hours, I finally succumb to the dark and Angel is the last thing on my mind. I slept through the day and into the night, awakening only when the hammering of a fist on my bedroom door jolted me up from my restless sleep.

My dreams had been filled with Angel and her agony and some disturbing qualities that baffle me. Late, I jump from the bed, shower, dress in record time and impatiently wait for my coffeemaker to brew while I inhale some crappy frosted cereal. Once done, I race to the desk to relieve whomever is sitting there.

I was anxious to return to the feed and make sure Angel is okay.

Shocking news meets me immediately, and from the time I return to my desk before sunup, the whole atmosphere in this shitty little house that I live and work in is been almost thick with unease.

The notes left from the last officer on shift states that Angel had been up since I passed out and she hadn't fallen to sleep until just a few hours ago. They further state that she had begun tearing the padding from the walls and the blankets from the windows late in the evening, and had been acting strangely enough to warrant concern.

Taylor wrote that she had peeled off her clothing and gyrated in front of the camera, giving him more of a view than he was prepared for and then a show that was of a pornographic nature.

"*Angel is staring right into it as if she knows it is there and she knows that I'm watching,*" I am actually a little bit jealous.

Taylor went on to say that that she stood naked afterwards, staring out the window at the river for most of the early hours, masturbating and crying hysterically. She said only one word, twice; Leviathan. That name again.

The second time she said it, the video shows Angel smiling into the camera again, and masturbating with a toy that looked too large to be comfortable, though she seemed to be managing just fine. I would love to ask him more but Taylor keeled over and died from an aneurism at 04:33 this morning. Our supervisor called him in DRT - Dead Right There.

I've been through two pots of coffee since and Angel is just now rising.

She comes awake early, sitting up with a stretch and wearing an opaque tee that turns nearly transparent in the light through the uncovered window. A porn star moan escapes her lips that makes more than the hair on my neck stand on end. Normally, she wakes up with a gasping scream and with her fingers clawing at her throat.

She is quiet too, not humming some obscure Leonard Cohen tune under her breath or blasting death metal loud enough to mute her rambling. Her tastes in music often cause me to look up the artists she listens to and surprisingly enough, I like most of it. I don't like this change in behaviour though. It leaves me cold.

7

Angel seems off, and has from the moment she rose and went about her morning routine. Other than the obvious changes, the subtler ones are more disturbing, in my opinion.

For instance, the way, she keeps pausing to stare out the kitchen window with her fingers quivering on the tattered remains of a drape. She had avoided the area like the plague when it was covered and now she stands there openly with an unobstructed view. I am sure she is watching for him.

There have been no further disruptions by the man who hammered on her door the other day, and no one has seen him around since either.

I'd like to think that he took himself off to whatever circle of hell he ran away from, but I doubt it. These types rarely give up that easily.

The woman who appeared so afraid the first time I saw her, is dancing in her living room and singing I Touch Myself by the Divinyls at the top of her lungs and it should make me smile, watching her have fun. It doesn't though and I'm not sure why.

Angel comes close to the camera and sings directly into it, running her hands across her ample breasts and down her hips suggestively. *I touch myself, I honestly do* - her lips form the words and my pants are suddenly a little tighter. I am desperate for her to leave for wherever she goes during the day so that I can relieve this tension and maybe rest if I can. I've taken a double shift considering the recent tragedy and being overtired is not helping in the least, most certainly not when it comes to my baser needs.

Angel left later than usual, taking extra time to fuss over her hair before bolting out the door. I slept most of the day while she was out and my dreams were surreal and blatantly sexual. I had admitted to myself quite a while ago that I wanted her, but it was an impossibility and so I tried to forget about it, ignore it but this dream was so real that I sat up howling with my thigh covered in cum and sweating as though I'd run the miracle mile.

Why I was I dreaming of Angel bound and on her knees while I skullfucked her perfect moaning lips, of tying her to the spare bed and banging her like a screen door in a windstorm? Vaguely embarrassed, I grabbed for the kleenex box on the nightstand and wiped away the wetness.

I hadn't had a wet dream since the one about Penny Dean in the 10th grade and quite like that one, this episode had me not only confused, but horny as hell.

It is worrisome; the whole situation is frankly a mess that I don't know how to get out of. It hadn't been that long since I'd had sex, a couple of weeks at best and Angel is intangible. I know this, as well as the fact that she is broken in ways that I can't even begin to imagine trying to repair, although I would just about kill for the opportunity to try. I'd murder the world just to see her smile without that edge of fear. I may have to –

It comes down to the fact that I can't abandon her and I've played over and over the few options on a continuous loop. Sadly, I'm still no closer to a solution as I was on that first day.

While I shower and inhale a frozen pizza, my mind worries at the issue like a rabid dog and I am just sitting back down at the desk with a bottle of Dr. Pepper in my hand when she walks through the front door.

Angel's hair is down and curling prettily against her shoulders. The top four buttons of her white blouse are open and I can see the pink lace of her bra peeking against the swell of her ample breast.

Jesus, I need a vacation.
I need her.
I think I'm going insane.

"Calvin Moon." Angel surprises me by speaking not to her daemons but to directly me, and that honey over whiskey voice makes my name sound like decadent treat on her tongue; exotic and so plainly erotic that my guts throb when she drops the skirt and the pristine chemise follows suit.

I'm suddenly sure that I will die with an epic hard on and the bluest balls any man has ever witnessed.

Every part of her is perfect, down to the small round marks that dot the porcelain landscape of her flesh and the ugly snarl of scar that mars her smooth belly.

This isn't happening.

Her pretty prismatic eyes stare straight back at me while I splutter and glance around, hoping that someone else is there but I am alone and I know that too. I'm also sporting a boner that could put someone's eye out.

The smile on her lips puts Mona Lisa to shame and is almost as enigmatic; I am devastated to see her lovely lips turning down into a trembling bow before she gives a deep hearted sigh.

"Calvin Moon. Cal, you naughty boy, I know that you are watching and I know you like what you see.

You can have it, all of this, as often and in as many ways as you want, but there is something you should know. Your Angel is a devil. I don't think it really matters to you though. Its not about the mind but the body for you creatures."

I don't know how to respond but seem helpless not to stroke myself as I watch her undulate and not move at the same time. The thing that was once Angel croons in a sing song voice that is an atrocity and something I think I could listen to for the rest of my life.

"Calvin! I do like being inside her like this. Wouldn't you like to be too? Taylor wanted it so badly he died with his dick in his hands. You're stronger than he was. Come on Calvin, come find me. I'll even give you a hint. *Hell is Empty.*"

This isn't Angel; it may wear her flesh and speak with her voice but there is no way that the woman that I have fallen into something more than like with has ever spoke or acted in this way. If the words coming from her pretty lips weren't enough evidence, the black rash that was creeping across her neck and shoulders was. The woman who was once Angel capers and gyrates, calling my name in a way that makes my spine crawl and God help me, I want to go to her.

"I can hear your thoughts Calvin Moon. I can hear in your mind how much you want to be inside this body, and you can be, if you find me. Can you, Cal? I gave you a hint and I never do that. I like you Calvin. I want you as much as you want me."

I can. Of course I can. I do, God help me, I do but first I had to know something more.

She almost got her claws in me, but I remembered the notes and the name Angel had said while staring out at the river said.

I called it back at the monster wearing the beautiful costume of a woman I almost knew.

"Leviathan. That's your name, isn't it? Leviathan? What's wrong sweetheart, now that I know your name you are afraid of little old me?"

It freezes in the middle of its gleeful dance and hisses back at the camera with its hands up in front of Angel's gorgeous face. I have it where I want it, and I call its name once more with a command that I hadn't been aware I possessed.

Her eyes sparkle with deadly life, and Angel's captor nods vigorously, agreeing to the terms that I blurt out in desire. She is going to be mine but first I have a few ends to tie up.

8

The first step was easy enough. A short, urgent text to my supervisor with her address was enough to cause a full team of amped up, armed and riot gear dressed men to fly toward where what was once Leviathan jumps up and down clapping its hands in happiness.

The next step was for my new love to take care of, and she flitters about smashing and destroying most of the belongings in the small apartment. The scene had to look realistic and Leviathan was doing a bang-up job.

My phone chimes and I see a text from the boss saying that they are enroute to her apartment. "Levi, it's time to go. Remember what I told you."

A large toothsome grin mars her face and she disintegrates as outside the door of the apartment above the Empty Hell Bar and Grill bursts open. Loud male voices shout moments before they explode into the room. Confused, they stand stunned for a moment and I can see the wide-eyed recognition of fear and knowledge fill their faces in the seconds before the blast.

Sadly, the firestorm took most of the building, its tenants, and the men that had come to rid us of the thing that had infested Angel's body. Leviathan ran amok for a brief time, and during its reign, it chose to rid the world of anyone left alive that knew about it. Thankfully, I was spared the horror of observing Leviathan's glee. Watching the aftermath on the television was sufficient enough for me.

Truly, the carnage was a terrible loss for the city and for its residents, and I felt badly for a long time about the lives that had been taken in the name of keeping humanity safe. But that was then.

Now

During my waking hours, I mourn and try to make amends by volunteering at the local soup kitchens and providing psychological care for some of the free clinics in my area as well. It's a small sacrifice for a larger cause and although it does little good, it makes that lump in my chest hurt less.

In the daytime, everything seems so regular and lives are returning to normal. I don't enjoy the sunlight anymore and find myself yearning for the comfort of the night. Winter brings the relief of darkness early and tonight is no exception.

Tonight, the clock is moving so exceptionally slow, creeping instead of racing and I can't help but watch the minutes creep by.

The clinic where I currently work is all but empty and my last patient is rambling on about some woman in red that dances outside his bedroom window at midnight, and how she wants to eat his soul.

He is half right anyway; she doesn't want his soul but she does want to devour him in an effort to slake that hunger that grows exponentially.

My text tone chimes, letting me know that time is finally up and that my wife needs me to bring something home. My poor darling is starving and craving something a little bit special. She can't help what the baby wants, can she?

"Peter, our time is up for this week but why don't you come home with me tonight? Angel and I would love to have you for dinner."

ABOUT THE AUTHOR

Melanie McCurdie is a North American horror fiction author and poet who resides in Tennessee. She is the warrior mother of two challenging boys, a poet and a blogger. Melanie is a supporter of indie film and publication, and is a devout horror junkie with a taste for words and blood sauce.

Most recently, Melanie was voice talent to The Carmen Theatre Group as Maria Sanchez and she can be seen in The Orphan Killer 2: Bound x Blood, written and created by Matt Farnsworth.

Made in the USA
Lexington, KY
20 May 2019